This Journal Belongs To:

My camp name:

My cabin:

My Cabin Notes:

My Counselor:

Camp Counselors:

Funny Nicknames:

Camp Songs:

I Saw Animals:

I Saw Bugs:

Activities List:

My Favourite Activity:

Cool Stuff I Made:

Favourite Camp Food:

Letters And Surprises From Home:

Scary Stories:

Funny Stories:

I Saw Stars And Constellations:

Fun Around The Campfire:

What I Learned About Nature:

At Camp, I Learned How To:

_____

_____

_____

_____

_____

_____

_____

_____

_____

_____

_____

_____

_____

_____

_____

_____

_____

_____

_____

_____

_____

_____

My Favourite Camp Memory:

_____

_____

_____

_____

_____

_____

_____

_____

_____

_____

_____

_____

_____

_____

_____

_____

_____

_____

_____

_____

_____

_____

_____

My New BFFs:

What Happens At Camp Stays At Camp:

What I Missed About Home:

I Forgot To Pack:

I Hurt Myself Doing:

Daily Weather Report:

I Am Grateful For:

Autographs:

Random Thoughts: